for John, Martina, Sophie, and Gemma Aston—
    and Paddy

Our Puppy's Vacation

RUTH BROWN

E. P. DUTTON   NEW YORK

First published in the United States by E. P. Dutton,
2 Park Avenue, New York, N.Y. 10016,
a division of NAL Penguin Inc.

Originally published in Great Britain by Andersen Press Limited,
62–65 Chandos Place, London WC2N 4NW.

Printed in Hong Kong
First American Edition   OBE   10 9 8 7 6 5 4 3 2

Library of Congress Cataloging-in-Publication Data
Brown, Ruth.
    Our puppy's vacation.
    Summary: A puppy enjoys playing at the beach,
climbing hills, and making friends on her first
vacation.
    [1. Dogs—Fiction]   I. Title.
PZ7.B816980u   1987   [E]   87-5433
ISBN 0-525-44326-6

It was our puppy's first vacation.

Everything was new to her—
the wide, wide beach,

the screeching gulls,

and the crashing waves.

She played hide-and-seek,

follow the leader,

and leapfrog,

and another game of hide-and-seek,

this time with a difference!

There were things to eat

and drink.

There were hills to climb

and walls to climb.

But an old tree was a problem for her

in more ways than one.

She made friends—sometimes easily,

sometimes not so easily.

She was having such a good time

that she just wanted to go on playing

and playing,

even in the dark.

And that was only the first day!